The Littlest Rabbit

a little love story

This book belongs to

Megan Connolly

Happy Easter 1995!
Love,
Kara

Text and compilation Copyright © 1994 Michelle Lovric
Illustrations Copyright © 1994 Royle Publications Ltd

This edition published by Longmeadow Press
201 High Ridge Road, Stamford, Connecticut 06904

Design and Color Reproduction by Camway Autographics.
Set in Utopia

Library of Congress Cataloging-in-Publication Data
ISBN 0 - 681 - 45442 - 3
First Longmeadow Press Edition
0 9 8 7 6 5 4 3 2 1

Royle

Produced by Royle Publications Ltd, Royle House, Wenlock Road, London N1 7ST, England.
Created by Michelle Lovric, 53 Shelton Street, Covent Garden, London WC2H 9HE, England.
Printed and bound in Singapore

The Littlest Rabbit

a little love story

illustrated by Gillian Roberts
story by Michelle Lovric

LONGMEADOW
PRESS

It was Mother's Day, and all the little rabbits lined up to give their gifts to Mama.

4

Mama was very happy with her presents,
and with her baby bunnies.

"Now tell us a story, Mama"
said the little rabbits.

"Well," said Mama, "Once upon a time I was as little as you - no, littler, because I was always the littlest rabbit around - the littlest in my burrow, the littlest in my field, the littlest in my school. You know, it isn't much fun to be the littlest rabbit.

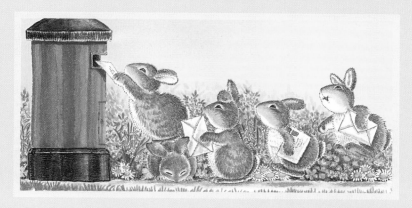

"The other rabbits made me do all the things they didn't want to do. When they wanted to mail a letter, I was the one at the bottom while the others climbed up to the top of the mailbox.

"When we were skating,
I was always dragged along at the end.

"I was the one the others jumped over, when they played leap frog.

"I was little, but I had some big ideas. I used to daydream all the time about what I would do when I grew up. One day I fell asleep and I had a strange dream.

"And in my dream there came a magic white rabbit. He said I could have one wish and that it could be whatever I wanted," said Mama.

"What did you wish?" asked the little rabbits.

"Well," said Mama, "I couldn't decide. Firstly I wanted to be a grownup and then I also wanted someone to play with who was *even smaller than I was*, but I also wanted to have an *adventure*.

"But the magic rabbit laughed and he said: 'But, little rabbit, you can have all those things: one first, and then the others: just wait and see'.

"And then he disappeared.

"When I woke up, it was magically my birthday - and I was grown up! I was wearing a party hat and behind me was a big present wrapped with a pink bow.

"Suddenly the present began to make strange noises!

"Then it burst open and a big, handsome rabbit jumped out.

"'Well,' I thought, 'this rabbit isn't *smaller* than I am, so he must be my *adventure!*'

"And that is exactly what he was.

"From the moment I saw him,
I felt such a strange feeling inside.
It was like birthday and Christmas and Easter all
mixed up, but better and a little bit scary.

"'Are you my adventure?' I asked him.

"'My name is Hugo,' he said. 'I don't know if I am your adventure, but I have brought you a picnic'.

"'Where shall we eat it?' I asked.

"'Ah,' said Hugo, 'I am going to take you to my secret island. We shall go there by boat'.

"When we arrived, we unpacked the picnic.
Then I saw that there was a birthday cake in the
shape of a heart.

"So we sat down and ate all the cake.
We climbed to the top of the
hill and watched the sun go down.

"The next day Hugo came with a big bunch of flowers and a present under his arm.

"'Now I have to go away for a few days to see my uncle,' he said.

"Then he gave me the present. 'And this box of chocolates is for you, too. Eat one each day and by the time they are gone I will be back'.

"So he packed his bags and went.
I waved him goodbye.

"I missed him.

"Every day I ate one chocolate.
Then one day a card arrived.

18

"It said: 'My darling little rabbit,
meet me at the Island on Thursday.
I have a surprise for you!'

"I went to the Island to find.....

"Your papa! In a new red bow tie!
With a big heart shaped box and a red rose.

"'Will you marry me?' asked Hugo.

"'Yes!' I said.

"So we were married. He wore a blue bow tie with white polka dots and I wore a pink ribbon.

"'What a wonderful adventure this has been,'
I told Hugo that night.

"'The magic rabbit has given me two wonderful
wishes. But I wonder when I will have someone
smaller to play with?' I said.

"Well, I did not have too long to wait as it turned out.

"Because not much later guess what happened?

"And now I have four little friends to play with."

"And Papa" said the baby rabbits.

"Yes, and Papa" said Mama, smiling!

The end.